Ho, Ho, Ho!

"How did you know my name was Jessica?" she asked the new custodian. She had been sent to his office to get the spare key to the art closet in Mrs. Otis's classroom.

Chris chuckled. "I have my ways," he answered. He handed her a candy cane. "Here's an early Christmas present for you."

"Thanks," Jessica whispered. As she turned to leave, she looked back. "You know what?"

Chris raised his bushy white eyebrows. "Yes?" he said.

"You look just like Santa Claus," Jessica told him.

"I do?" Chris said, laughing a "Ho, ho, ho" laugh. "Well, maybe I am Santa Cl—

Bantam Skylark Books in the
SWEET VALLEY KIDS series
Ask your bookseller for the
  books you have missed

SWEET VALLEY KIDS

SUPER SNOOPER

THE CASE OF THE SECRET SANTA

Written by
Molly Mia Stewart

Created by
FRANCINE PASCAL

Illustrated by
Ying-Hwa Hu

A BANTAM SKYLARK BOOK
NEW YORK · TORONTO · LONDON · SYDNEY · AUCKLAND

To Caitlin Molly Walsh

RL 2, 005–008

THE CASE OF THE SECRET SANTA

A Bantam Skylark Book / December 1990

*Sweet Valley High® and Sweet Valley Kids are trademarks of
Francine Pascal*

Conceived by Francine Pascal

*Produced by Daniel Weiss Associates, Inc.
33 West 17th Street
New York, NY 10011*

Cover art by Susan Tang

*Skylark Books is a registered trademark of Bantam Books, a division of
Bantam Doubleday Dell Publishing Group, Inc.*

ISBN 0-553-15860-0

Published simultaneously in the United States and Canada

---

*Bantam Books are published by Bantam Books, a division of Bantam
Doubleday Dell Publishing Group, Inc. Its trademark, consisting of the
words "Bantam Books" and the portrayal of a rooster, is Registered in U.S.
Patent and Trademark Office and in other countries. Marca Registrada.
Bantam Books, 666 Fifth Avenue, New York, New York 10103.*

PRINTED IN THE UNITED STATES OF AMERICA

CWO   0 9 8 7 6 5 4 3 2 1

CHAPTER 1

The New Club

Jessica Wakefield and her twin sister Elizabeth were playing on the jungle gym on Thursday afternoon. They were discussing a mystery book by Amanda Howard that Elizabeth had just finished. "Then what happened?" Jessica asked.

"When they found the last clue, they were able to read the secret message and solve the mystery," Elizabeth answered.

Amanda Howard was Elizabeth's favorite author. Elizabeth loved to read. She also liked to make up adventure games to play outside with her friends Amy Sutton and Eva Simpson. Jessica didn't enjoy reading as much. Playing with her dolls and stuffed animals was what she liked most. She always did her homework at the last minute, unless she and Elizabeth did it together.

From the outside, the two girls looked exactly alike. They had long blond hair with bangs and blue-green eyes. When they wore identical outfits to school, their best friends in Mrs. Otis's second-grade class couldn't always tell them apart. The only way to be sure who was who was to look at their name bracelets.

Even though they liked different things, Jessica and Elizabeth were best friends. They loved sharing a bedroom and being in the same family. They even divided cookies right in half.

"I wish I could solve a mystery," Elizabeth said, looking at her sister.

"It would be exciting to be a detective," Jessica said as she hung upside down on one of the lower bars of the jungle gym. She looked around the park. Everything looked upside down to her. "Here come Lila and Ellen," she said. Lila Fowler and Ellen Riteman were Jessica's best friends after Elizabeth.

"Eva and Amy are here, too," Elizabeth said. They were Elizabeth's best friends after Jessica. "We could all be detectives," she added.

Someone began to laugh higher up on the jungle gym. Jessica looked up and saw Todd Wilkins and Winston Egbert. "What are you laughing at?" she demanded.

"We're spying on you," Winston answered.

"That's right. Just like real detectives," Todd added.

"Ha, ha, ha," Jessica said, pulling herself up to a sitting position.

Elizabeth climbed to a higher bar. "Hi, you two."

When the other girls came over and climbed up, they began talking about their holiday vacation.

"Do you do anything special when school is out?" Eva asked. Eva's family had moved to Sweet Valley from Jamaica earlier in the school year.

"We could come to the park every day," Amy suggested.

"We do that already," Elizabeth pointed out. She thought for a moment. "I know. We could have a club!"

4

"A secret club," Lila Fowler spoke up. "And we'll only let certain people join."

"Ooooh! Can we be in it, too?" Todd asked, laughing with Winston.

Jessica looked at Elizabeth and shrugged.

"Sure," Elizabeth said. She was thoughtful for a moment. Then she got a happy look on her face. "We can have a mystery club! And we can all be detectives!"

"Detectives?" Ellen asked. "I've never solved a mystery before."

"It'll be fun," Elizabeth said. "We can look for clues—"

"And take fingerprints," Jessica added. "I did that once. All you need is an ink pad."

Winston and Todd climbed down so they were all on the same level. "Do you think we'll find any criminals?" Winston asked.

"Maybe," Elizabeth said. "We may even get a reward."

Jessica was thinking fast. "Our club should have a name," she said. "And we should have a secret handshake."

Jessica and Elizabeth already had a secret promise sign they used with each other and with their brother, Steve. Having a secret signal for the club would be fun.

Everyone had a different idea about what the secret sign should be. Amy suggested making a fist and tapping each other on the knuckles.

"We can't tell anyone who isn't in our club what we're doing," Lila said. "And we can't use the secret handshake with anyone else."

"Who's going to be president?" Eva asked.

"I vote for Elizabeth," Todd said.

"I vote for Jessica," Ellen chimed in.

6

Elizabeth felt happy to be nominated, but she liked to do so many things with Jessica that she knew she'd feel bad if she won.

"You could both be president," Winston said.

"Co-presidents," Elizabeth agreed. She looked happy. "Now all we need to do is find a mystery."

CHAPTER 2

The Mystery Mystery

Everyone was silent.

"How *do* you find a mystery?" Jessica asked.

Winston looked puzzled. "You look for clues, I guess."

"I'm not sure I know what a clue is," Eva said.

Elizabeth tried to remember all the Amanda Howard stories she had read. "Clues are the things that help you solve a mystery. They can be footprints or secret messages written in code," she said.

Amy frowned. "I don't know any codes," she said. "Does that mean I can't be in the club?"

"Of course you can," Elizabeth answered. "None of us know any codes."

Jessica spoke up. "What we need first is a mystery. Then we can begin to look for clues."

"I know a mystery!" Todd said excitedly.

Everyone looked at him. "My new baseball glove disappeared," he continued. "It vanished without a trace."

"I lost a doll," Ellen added.

"My mom says socks always get lost in our washing machine," Winston said.

Elizabeth frowned. "Those don't sound like real mysteries to me."

Lila began to smile. "I know. We can all find out what we're getting for Christmas. I already know some of the presents I'm getting."

Everyone started talking at once. Elizabeth was worried that they would never become real detectives if they couldn't agree on anything. "Quiet, everyone!" she shouted.

They all stopped talking and looked at her. "We have to think about finding a mystery to solve," she reminded them.

"The mystery is *what is* the mystery," Jessica said with a giggle.

Eva was sitting quietly on one of the bars. "I thought of a name," she said shyly. "We could be the Snoopers Club."

"The Snoopers Club," Elizabeth repeated. "That sounds good." The others nodded in agreement. "From now on, all the members of the Snoopers Club—Amy, Eva, Lila, Ellen, Todd, Winston, Jessica, and me—

10

should be on the lookout for a mystery. OK? Let's have our first meeting tomorrow at recess."

Every one of the Snoopers nodded. Then they climbed down from the jungle gym and tried out their secret handshake. Elizabeth smiled happily. She was sure the Snoopers Club was going to find a mystery and solve it.

When Elizabeth and Jessica rode their bikes home from the park, Elizabeth was still thinking about mysteries. "Maybe we could find a hidden treasure," she said.

"I bet there's some at home," Jessica said. She lowered her voice. "Like Christmas presents."

Elizabeth gasped. "You're not supposed to look for them," she said.

"I know," Jessica answered. "Besides, most

11

of them come from Santa Claus. And those won't be delivered until Christmas Eve. I sure hope I'm on Santa's list again this year."

"Come on, Jessica," Elizabeth said. "We're too old to believe in Santa anymore. Mom and Dad buy all the presents."

Jessica's eyes widened. "Really? I thought Santa was real."

"Well, I don't believe in him anymore," Elizabeth announced. Until last Christmas, she had believed in Santa Claus, too. But now she was older and thought Santa was just a made-up story for young children. But her sister still believed in him.

"I hope Santa brings me new leotards and a Little Linda doll," Jessica continued, ignoring what Elizabeth had said. "And a stuffed pony and a watch that glows in the dark like Lila's."

13

"Well, if there is a Santa, I wish he would bring me a real pony," Elizabeth said. "We could keep it in the backyard. I'd name it Lightning."

Jessica made a face. "Real ponies take a lot of work, Liz," she complained.

"Well Santa isn't real anyway so he won't bring me a real pony," Elizabeth said.

"He *is* real," Jessica said angrily. She pedaled her bike a little way ahead.

Elizabeth frowned. If Jessica wanted to keep believing in Santa Claus, that was all right with her. But that didn't mean she had to believe in him, too.

CHAPTER 3

Ho, ho, ho!

The next day was Friday, and Mrs. Otis made an announcement right after she took attendance.

"We're going to decorate our classroom," she told everyone. "We'll put up Christmas and Hanukkah decorations for our holiday party next week."

Jessica was very happy. That meant no spelling!

"I need a volunteer," the teacher went on.

Caroline Pearce shot her hand up. She always wanted to be the teacher's pet. "I'll help, Mrs. Otis," she said, waving her arm.

"Thank you, Caroline. You can hand out art supplies," Mrs. Otis said. "I need one more volunteer. Jessica?"

Jessica stood up. "Should I get the art supplies?" she said, heading toward the back of the room.

"No, Jessica," Mrs. Otis said. "Would you please go to the custodian's office and get the spare key to the large closet. I misplaced my key and that's where the decorations from last year are. Jim will give you the key."

Jessica felt lucky. It was fun going on errands when everyone else was in class. She ran out to the hallway and then dawdled, peeking in the glass panels of the other doors. The students were busy doing class-work. It made Jessica feel special.

When she got to the custodian's office, the door was open. "Jim?" she called.

"Come in," said an unfamiliar voice.

Jessica looked inside. Instead of the regular janitor, she saw someone she had never seen before. He was an elderly, jolly-looking man with white hair and a white beard. He was looking at a piece of paper in his hand, but when Jessica entered, he put the paper down and gave her a friendly wave.

"Come on in! Jim isn't here. But what can I do for you, young lady?" he asked cheerfully.

"I need the spare key for the large closet in Mrs. Otis's second grade room," Jessica told him. She took a step closer and looked at the piece of paper he was holding. She could see many columns of names on it. "Who are all those people?"

The man smiled. "Oh, just friends of mine," he said with a wink. "I'm making presents for them, and I was just going over the list to make sure I haven't left anyone out."

"You sure have a lot of friends," Jessica said.

"I certainly do," he answered with a chuckle. He opened a table drawer and took out a ring of keys. Each one had a tag on it. "I'll find you that key in just a minute," he said. "I'm filling in for Jim for a bit. My name is Chris."

Chris held out his hand. Jessica was surprised, but she shook his hand just like a grown-up. Then she waited while Chris sorted through the keys. "Here we are," he said finally, holding up a key.

"Thank you," Jessica said.

19

"You're very welcome, Jessica," Chris replied.

Jessica blinked. "How did you know my name was Jessica?" she asked in surprise.

"Maybe I guessed it," Chris said. His eyes twinkled with laughter. "And I guess that you have a sister, too."

"That's right," Jessica said, nodding slowly.

"Named Elizabeth?" Chris went on.

Jessica stared at him. "How did you know?"

Chris chuckled. "I have my ways," he said. He opened another drawer and took out a candy cane. "Here's an early Christmas present for you."

"Thanks," Jessica whispered. She was so puzzled she didn't know what else to say. Chris was very mysterious, but he was so nice she liked him anyway.

As Jessica turned around to leave, she looked back. "You know what?" she said.

Chris raised his bushy white eyebrows. "Yes?" he said.

"You look just like Santa Claus," Jessica told him.

"I do?" Chris said. "Well, maybe I am Santa Claus."

Jessica giggled. "No, you're not," she said in a scolding tone. "Santa Claus lives at the North Pole."

Chris laughed loudly. It sounded like he was saying "Ho, ho, ho!" Jessica smiled and waved good-bye. It was time to get back to her class. And she couldn't wait to talk to the other members of the Snoopers Club. She had found a mystery!

CHAPTER 4

The Snoopers' First Case

Elizabeth looked over her shoulder to see if anyone was following. "The coast is clear," she whispered to the other Snoopers.

The group hurried across the playground and stopped under a large tree. No one was nearby.

"OK," Elizabeth said. "This is our first official Snoopers meeting. Has anyone found a mystery yet?"

Amy shook her head. "I can't think of a single mystery."

"Neither can I," Ellen said.

"Maybe we need a different kind of club," Winston suggested.

"No!" Jessica shouted.

Elizabeth could tell her sister had something exciting to tell the group. Jessica always had a special look in her eyes when she had a secret.

"What is it?" Elizabeth asked.

Jessica looked around at the others. She had a big grin on her face. "You're not going to believe this," she began in a quiet voice, "but I think Santa Claus himself is here at our school."

"What?" Todd yelled.

Lila began to laugh. "No way," Winston said. Everyone shook their heads and started teasing Jessica.

Elizabeth was staring at her sister. "What are you talking about?" she asked.

23

Jessica raised her chin stubbornly and waited for the others to stop laughing. "When I went to the custodian's office," she explained, "I met our new janitor. His name is Chris. He has white hair and a beard just like Santa Claus, and he was looking at a list of people who are going to get gifts, just like Santa's supposed to."

"So what?" Lila said. "My father has a long list of people to give presents to, but that doesn't make him Santa Claus."

Ellen and Amy laughed.

"That's not all!" Jessica shouted. She looked angry. "He knew my name without me telling him. How did he do that?"

Elizabeth frowned. She had to agree that that was puzzling. Then she smiled. "Look," she said, holding up Jessica's arm. "He probably saw your name bracelet."

24

"Oh." Jessica looked disappointed, but she wasn't giving up. "He also knew I had a sister named Elizabeth," she said. "He didn't see your name bracelet, because you weren't even there. So how did he know your name, Miss Smarty?"

"All our names are on our cubbies," Todd answered for Elizabeth. "And you two have your cubbies right next to each other. He could have seen them when he was cleaning our classroom."

Elizabeth smiled at Todd. "That's right."

"Do you *still* think he's Santa Claus?" Ellen teased.

"Well, I don't know," Jessica mumbled.

"He isn't, Jessica," Todd said. "Why would Santa Claus come to our school?"

"Yeah!" the others chimed in.

"Besides, Santa's not a janitor," Winston pointed out.

Jessica crossed her arms. "Maybe I'm wrong, but I still think Chris could be Santa."

Elizabeth thought it was silly to spend the whole Snoopers meeting talking about Santa Claus. "Listen everyone," she said. "We still don't have a mystery to solve."

"We do, too," Jessica said. "We have to find out whether or not our new custodian is really Santa Claus!"

"But Santa isn't real anyway," Elizabeth said.

No one said a word. Elizabeth looked around at the group. "Right?" she asked.

Todd agreed. "I don't believe in Santa anymore," he said.

"What about you, Eva?" Jessica asked. "Do you believe in Santa?"

Eva looked at the others, and then nodded slowly. "Yes, I do. In Jamaica we called him Father Christmas."

"I believe in him, too," Ellen said. Lila shook her head no. But Amy nodded that she did believe in Santa Claus.

Elizabeth was surprised. Almost everyone believed in Santa except her. "Winston?" she asked.

Winston looked embarrassed. "I'm pretty sure I believe in Santa," he admitted.

"Then that's what our mystery should be," Jessica said firmly. "We have to find out if Chris is Santa Claus. Raise your hand if you agree with me."

Five hands went up. Only Elizabeth, Todd, and Lila didn't vote. The three of them looked at each other and shrugged. They didn't have any other mysteries to solve, so they were going to go along with this one.

"This is our first case," Jessica said happily. "I can't wait to get started!"

CHAPTER 5

Clue Number One

Jessica was beginning to feel very excited. It was the Snoopers' first mystery, and she had found it! "We need to find out more about Chris," she told the others. "Who wants to go with me to the principal's office?"

Lila gave her a smile. "I will. But I don't think we'll find out anything."

"OK," Jessica said. She didn't pay any attention to Lila's know-it-all tone of voice.

"Try to find out his whole name," Annie suggested.

"And if he lives at the North Pole," Elizabeth said with a giggle.

Todd laughed. "I'll go look in the parking lot to see if there's a sleigh and reindeer parked outside."

Jessica didn't care if Elizabeth and Todd were making fun of her. She was going to find out if Chris was really Santa Claus.

Jessica and Lila ran into the school building and walked quickly down the hall to Mrs. Armstrong's office.

"Don't let anyone know what we're doing," Jessica whispered. "This is our club secret."

Lila nodded. "No one will believe us anyway," she said with a grin.

"Just because you don't think Chris could be Santa doesn't mean no one else would," Jessica said angrily. "I think it's a good mystery. Besides, it's the only one we've found."

"I'm sorry, Jess," Lila told her. "I think it's a good mystery, too."

Jessica nodded. "OK. Let's go."

The two girls went into the principal's office. A secretary was typing a letter while Mrs. Armstrong was reading a memo.

"Hi, girls," she said with a smile. "What can I do for you?"

Jessica looked at Lila. "Umm . . . I was talking to Chris, the new janitor," she began.

"Chris Kreeger?" Mrs. Armstrong asked. "What about him?"

Jessica could hardly believe her ears. Chris Kreeger? Chris Kreeger sounded very much like Kris Kringle, which was one of the names for Santa Claus. She stared at Lila. Lila looked surprised, too.

"We were wondering," Lila said, "if he was from Sweet Valley?"

Mrs. Armstrong smiled. "You know, it's funny you should ask me that question, because he came from far away. He said he just moved here from Alaska."

"Alaska?" Jessica repeated, her eyes growing wide. Alaska was very close to the North Pole! That was a very important clue.

"Why are you asking all these questions about the new custodian?" Mrs. Armstrong asked them.

Jessica thought fast. "He looks like someone my mom knows," she answered, crossing her fingers behind her back. She hoped she wouldn't get in trouble for saying something that wasn't true. Then she remembered that if Chris Kreeger was Santa and he found out that she had lied, he might take her off his list! "I was just curious," she added.

"Well, he's a very nice gentleman," Mrs. Armstrong said. "And we're very happy to have him. Now why don't you girls go on back outside? It's still recess."

Lila tugged at Jessica's sleeve as they walked quickly down the hall. "Did you hear that?" she whispered. "He lived in Alaska!"

"I know!" Jessica gasped. "We have to tell the rest of the Snoopers."

"And then we have to find more clues," Lila said. She was suddenly very excited about the case.

The two girls started running. Everything was getting more mysterious by the second!

CHAPTER 6

Santa's Clothes

Elizabeth listened carefully as Jessica and Lila told the others what Mrs. Armstrong had said. Both girls were breathing hard from running all the way back outside.

"Don't you think that's an important clue?" Jessica demanded when they were done.

"Just because he used to live in Alaska doesn't mean he's Santa Claus," Todd said.

Amy glared at him. "If he looks like Santa and sounds like Santa and lived near the North Pole, I think he *is* Santa Claus."

"I think we still need more clues," Elizabeth decided. "Maybe we could explore the custodian's office."

Everyone was quiet for a moment. "Do you think Chris might be eating lunch?" Eva asked.

"There's only one way to find out," Winston said. "Let's go check."

The Snoopers ran inside and raced for the custodian's office. Elizabeth wasn't sure about Chris being Santa Claus, but she, too, was curious. Even if Chris Kreeger wasn't Santa Claus, he seemed very mysterious, and she wanted to know more about him.

Everyone slowed down. Jessica tiptoed to the door and knocked softly. Elizabeth held her breath.

There was no answer. Jessica turned the knob and opened the door. She peeked inside. "The place is empty," she whispered.

One by one, the Snoopers entered the room. There was a large metal cabinet, metal shelves filled with cleaning supplies, a ladder, some buckets and brooms, a small table and chair, and several closets. A large comfortable chair was in the center of the room.

"What do we do?" Ellen asked. She looked nervous and excited at the same time.

"Let's look for clues," Elizabeth said.

"And everyone be quiet," Jessica added. "We don't want anyone to know we're here."

The boys and girls spread out and began to examine everything in the room. Nobody made any noise, except when Winston bumped into a metal pail. It made a clanging noise in the quiet room.

"Shhh!" Elizabeth whispered. She looked at the list of telephone numbers on the wall: plumber, electrician, carpenter—

"LOOK!" Todd said in a breathless voice.

Everyone stopped what they were doing. Todd had opened one of the closets. Hanging inside was a Santa Claus suit!

"Oh my gosh," Amy said. "He is Santa!"

Elizabeth was so surprised that she didn't know what to say. The others were all talking excitedly. Jessica looked very happy. "I was right from the beginning," she said proudly.

"Let me see that suit," Elizabeth said.

Todd took the red Santa coat off the hanger and tried it on. The sleeves hung down over his hands. "Ho, ho, ho!" he said.

"Put that back," Winston said quickly. "You're not supposed to wear Santa's clothes!"

Elizabeth looked closely at the coat. It was bright red with white trimming, large

pockets, and a wide black belt attached by belt loops. She stuck her hand into one of the pockets.

"Hey!" she gasped. "There's something here."

"Another clue?" Lila asked.

Elizabeth pulled out a piece of paper. She unfolded a letter that had "Charles Department Store" written across the top. That was the name of a store in the Sweet Valley mall. She read the letter quickly, and then laughed.

"Look," she said. "It says here that Mr. Kreeger was hired to be Santa Claus for the store's Santa's Toyshop. So, he's just *dressing up* as Santa Claus so little kids can sit on his lap and tell him what they want for Christmas."

Jessica frowned. "Let me see that," she

said and snatched the letter from Elizabeth. She read it carefully. "That still doesn't mean he's not the real Santa."

"Yeah," Ellen chimed in.

Winston hung up the Santa coat in the closet. "I know one way to find out," he said. The others looked at him. "We can all go to Charles Department Store tomorrow and ask him if he knows what we each want for Christmas."

CHAPTER 7

On Santa's Lap

Jessica rushed out to the car after breakfast on Saturday. "Hurry up, Liz!" she ordered.

"What's the big rush?" Mr. Wakefield asked once they were all inside. "You're very impatient this morning, Jessica."

"We have to find out if our new custodian at school is really Santa Claus," Jessica explained. "Elizabeth doesn't believe he is, and I do." She looked at Elizabeth and Elizabeth shook her head.

Their father looked at them in the rearview mirror and smiled. "What makes you think he's Santa Claus?" he asked them.

"Lots of reasons," Jessica said. She told him all the clues they had found. "So I'm positive it's him."

"I'm not," Elizabeth said. "I don't believe in Santa, anyway."

"I think you need to find a little more evidence," Mr. Wakefield said in a serious tone of voice. He was a lawyer, and his job was to prove things. "You need enough clues to prove your case beyond the shadow of a doubt."

Elizabeth laughed. "I have a big shadow of doubt."

Jessica stuck her tongue out at her sister. "You'll see. When we get to the mall, we'll find out more."

The rest of the Snoopers were all waiting

in front of Charles Department Store with their parents. Jessica noticed that most of the children waiting to see Santa Claus were much younger than they were. The Snoopers were definitely the oldest in line, but Jessica didn't care. She could see Chris in his Santa suit, sitting in a big chair at Santa's Toyshop. Jessica couldn't wait for her turn. "I'll bet you anything he'll know what I want for Christmas," she whispered to the others.

"I wrote him a letter two weeks ago and sent it to the North Pole," Ellen admitted. "Do you think he could have gotten it since he's here and not there?"

Jessica nodded. "You don't even have to send Santa a letter. He always knows what you want."

"How could he know?" Elizabeth asked. "Do you think he can read minds?"

"He just knows, that's all," Winston said confidently. "If Chris is Santa, he'll know."

"I think this is dumb," Todd said. He looked around and made a sour face. "There's no one here except little babies. And us."

The line moved slowly forward. Each child went up to Chris and sat on his lap while he talked to them. He laughed his big "Ho, ho, ho" laugh and made all the children in line giggle. One little boy tugged on Chris's beard to see if it was real, and that made Chris laugh even more. Each child looked very happy and excited as he or she got off his lap.

"It's your turn next," Lila whispered to Jessica.

As Jessica stepped up, Chris saw her and waved. "Well, hello there," he called out. "Come on up and let's have a chat. It's nice to see some of my friends from school."

Jessica smiled at the other Snoopers, then hurried up to Chris. She climbed onto his lap.

"Hello," she said. "I bet you're surprised to see me."

"Not at all," Chris answered. "I had a feeling you would come."

"You did?" Jessica whispered.

Chris nodded. "I love talking to all the kids," he went on cheerfully. "That's the best part of my job."

Jessica wasn't sure which job he meant. Did he mean being Santa at the store, or being a custodian at the school, or being Santa Claus for real?

She looked into his twinkly blue eyes. "Chris, are you really Santa Claus?" she asked in a serious tone.

"Do you believe in Santa Claus?" Chris asked her just as seriously.

"Yes," she said, nodding her head. "I do. But my sister Liz doesn't. Will you still bring her Christmas presents?"

"Ho ho ho!" Chris laughed. "Of course I will. I'll bet I know what she wants, too."

Jessica crossed her fingers behind her back. She hoped he would guess correctly.

"I bet she wants a pony," Chris whispered. His cheeks got as rosy as apples when he smiled. "Am I right?"

Jessica's eyes widened and she gulped. "Yes."

"And if I'm not mistaken, I think you'd like to have the Little Linda doll."

Jessica was so surprised she almost slid off his lap. "Yes, please!" she said. She jumped

49

down. "Thanks a lot, Chris. See you in school on Monday."

She ran back to the other Snoopers. "It's really Santa," she said. "He knew I wanted a Little Linda doll!"

"It's the most popular doll," Elizabeth pointed out. "It was a lucky guess."

Jessica pretended not to hear her sister. She was certain Chris was Santa Claus now, and nothing was going to change her mind.

CHAPTER 8

Santa is Real

"He guessed what Liz wants, and what Ellen wants, and Winston and Todd and me and everyone," Jessica said at dinner. She took a big gulp of milk.

"He sounds very smart," Mrs. Wakefield said.

"And he's perfect for the part," Mr. Wakefield added. "He's the most realistic Santa I ever saw."

Jessica smiled. "That's because he *is* the real Santa, Daddy."

"No way!" said Steven, the twins' older

brother. "A real Santa Claus! Ha, ha, ha!" he hooted. "Ho, ho, ho."

Jessica pointed her fork at him. "Don't make fun of him, Steven. You might not get any Christmas presents."

"I think I might," Steven said. "Two of Santa's helpers might get them for me," he added with a grin, looking at Mr. and Mrs. Wakefield.

Jessica ignored her brother. "Mom, Mrs. Otis said we could invite Chris to our class holiday party. She wanted to know if you would help by being a class mother."

Mrs. Wakefield served herself some salad while she thought about it. "Well, I guess I could. I think that would be fun."

"Hooray," Jessica said happily. "This is going to be the best Christmas ever. I'm so glad I finally got to meet the real Santa Claus."

Mr. and Mrs. Wakefield looked at each other. "Jessica," Mrs. Wakefield said. "You understand that Mr. Kreeger is not really Santa, don't you?"

"What do you mean?" Jessica demanded. "He is."

"He's a very nice man," Mr. Wakefield agreed. "He's jolly and he acts like Santa, but he is *not* Santa Claus."

Jessica shook her head. "Yes, he is," she said. Her parents just didn't understand.

Steven laughed. "You really believe in—"

"I'm not listening to you!" Jessica shouted. "You don't know anything." She put her hands over her ears and looked at Elizabeth.

Elizabeth was using her knife to push her peas around on her plate.

"Liz, you believe in him now, right?" Jessica asked.

Elizabeth shrugged. "Well, if I did believe in Santa, I guess I would believe Chris is Santa."

"Elizabeth!" Jessica cried out. She stood up and began counting off all the clues the Snoopers had found. "First of all, Chris Kreeger's name sounds almost like Kris Kringle. Second of all, he used to live near the North Pole. Third of all, he knows what presents we want. Fourth of all—"

"Fourth of all, you're nuts," Steven interrupted.

"That's enough, Steven," their father broke in. He looked at Jessica. "Honey, the clues may make it seem like Chris is Santa Claus, but I think they're just coincidences."

Jessica glared at her father. "How do *you* know?"

"I just know," he answered.

"When you're a little older, you'll understand," her mother added in a gentle voice.

Jessica shook her head. "You think that just because you're grown-ups you know everything. I believe that Chris is Santa Claus, no matter what you say." She stomped out of the dining room and went upstairs.

Elizabeth followed her. She quietly opened their bedroom door and sat down next to her sister. "Are you mad?" she asked.

"No," Jessica said. "They don't know Chris like we do. But I don't understand why you don't believe me."

Elizabeth frowned. "I'm sorry," she said

slowly. "But you heard Mom and Dad say there's no way he can be Santa Claus, and I don't think they would lie."

"They just don't know," Jessica explained. "But I do. Chris is Santa Claus. I'll prove it to you."

CHAPTER 9

The Party Invitation

"Hurry up!" Lila called, waving her arm.

Elizabeth and Jessica put their books on their school desks and ran to the back of the classroom for a quick meeting with the other Snoopers.

"What's going on?" Elizabeth asked.

Winston looked over his shoulder to make sure no one else in their class could hear them. "We want to be the ones to invite Chris to our class party," he whispered. "You and Jessica should ask Mrs. Otis."

"Why us?" Jessica asked.

"Because it was your idea and you're the co-presidents," Todd reminded them.

Elizabeth nodded. Mrs. Otis had already said that Chris could come to their Christmas and Hanukkah party, but no one had invited him yet.

"OK," she decided. "Maybe we have time before class starts."

Amy nudged Jessica with her elbow. "Go on. Ask Mrs. Otis."

"I'll go with you," Winston said.

Together, Elizabeth, Jessica, and Winston marched up to the teacher's desk. "Mrs. Otis?" Jessica said.

"Yes?" Mrs. Otis gave them a friendly smile.

"We want to be the ones to invite Chris to our party," Elizabeth explained. "Can we go now and ask him?"

Mrs. Otis looked surprised. "All three of you?" They nodded quickly. "I guess that would be fine. Hurry back, though."

"Come on," Elizabeth said. They ran down the hall to the custodian's office. The door was open when they arrived. Chris was sitting in the big chair.

"Chris?" Jessica said.

Chris turned around and smiled. "Visitors! Welcome."

The three of them filed in and stood around him. A large world map was spread out on a table.

"What's that for?" Winston asked.

Chris scratched his white beard. "I'm planning my route," he explained.

"Are you going away?" Elizabeth asked.

"I'm taking a trip," Chris told them. "I take a big trip every year, and I like to go a different way each time."

Jessica poked Elizabeth in the back. When Elizabeth looked at her, Jessica's eyes were wide. "A big trip!" Jessica whispered in Elizabeth's ear. "You know what that means!"

"It doesn't mean anything," Elizabeth whispered back.

Chris shifted in his chair and looked at Elizabeth. "I've heard you don't believe in Santa Claus. Is that true?"

"Yes," Elizabeth said slowly. "It's just a made up story to get little children in the spirit of Christmas."

"Elizabeth!" Jessica gasped. She looked embarrassed. "She didn't mean that," she told Chris.

Chris chuckled. "Maybe she did. But tell

me, what does the spirit of Christmas mean to you, Elizabeth?"

Elizabeth frowned while she thought. "Well, I guess it means that everyone is supposed to be kind and love each other. And people show their love by giving presents. But there's no Santa."

"Oh, brother," Jessica muttered. Winston's face was bright red.

"And what's wrong with believing in Santa?" Chris wanted to know.

"*I* believe in Santa," Jessica spoke up. "And I think you're him."

"You do?" Chris said with a big laugh.

Elizabeth put her hands on her hips. "If you're Santa, what are the names of the reindeer?"

"Hmmm . . . Let me think, now," Chris began.

Winston and Jessica held their breaths.

"There's Comet, Cupid, Donner, Vixen, Dasher, Dancer, Blitzen, and Prancer," Chris said, counting off on his fingers. "Oh, and of course, Rudolph."

"See?" Winston said. "He knows them all!"

"But I know them all, too," Elizabeth said. She looked at Chris. He wasn't smiling anymore, and Elizabeth began to worry that she was hurting his feelings.

"I'm sorry you don't believe in Santa Claus," Chris said sadly. "I always think that Santa Claus is one reason why Christmas is so special for children."

"Liz!" Jessica whispered angrily. "You're not being nice."

Elizabeth felt terrible. What if she was wrong? What if Santa Claus was real? What if Chris was Santa! After all he was kind and

64

friendly and cheerful, and he looked just like all the pictures of Santa Claus she had ever seen.

"I can't make you believe in Santa," Chris said gently. "But you do have the spirit of Christmas, and that's all that matters. Whether you believe in Santa is up to you," he added sadly.

Everyone was quiet. Winston was looking down at the floor, and Jessica looked disappointed. Elizabeth wondered if she had made a mistake.

"Well, you came here for a reason, didn't you?" Chris asked, smiling again.

"Oh, yes," Elizabeth said. "We wanted to invite you to our class party. It's tomorrow during recess."

"There'll be games and cake and everything," Winston added.

"Please?" Jessica asked. "We really, really want you to come."

Chris laughed his jolly "Ho, ho, ho" laugh. "I'm very glad you've asked me. I'll certainly be there. Now run along back to your class. Mrs. Otis will be wondering what kept you so long."

They nodded and left the office.

Jessica scolded her sister out in the hallway. "You were mean to him!"

Elizabeth hung her head. "I didn't mean to be," she said.

"Well, we just got two more clues that say he is Santa." Winston said.

Elizabeth didn't answer. She didn't know what to believe anymore.

CHAPTER 10

Is He or Isn't He?

On Tuesday morning, Elizabeth and Jessica put on their matching red dresses with white collars for the party. Jessica was so excited she couldn't sit still at breakfast.

"I can't believe Santa is coming to our party," she said happily. "It'll make it really special."

Mrs. Wakefield was packing party supplies in a shopping bag. "Santa?" she asked. "Do you mean someone dressed as Santa?"

"No, Santa Claus," Jessica said. "It's Chris, and he's coming to our party."

Elizabeth ate her cereal without saying anything. She was very confused about Chris.

"Now, Jessica, you know Mr. Kreeger isn't really Santa Claus," their mother said. "He just looks like him."

Jessica shook her head stubbornly. "He is Santa."

Elizabeth looked at her mother and shrugged. She wasn't sure of anything. Maybe Chris was Santa and maybe he wasn't. There was no way to be certain.

"Jessica—" Mrs. Wakefield began.

"I believe he's Santa," Jessica interrupted. "No matter what you say."

On the school bus, Jessica kept talking about their party. Elizabeth was deep in thought about the subject. It really was very mysterious. The Snoopers had found a lot of clues, but they didn't have any real proof.

Before the party began, the Snoopers all gathered together in a corner of the classroom. "Santa will be here any minute," Jessica said smiling.

"You mean Chris," Elizabeth corrected.

The others looked at her, but didn't say anything. They all looked a little bit doubtful.

"Let's go over our case," Todd said. "What are all the clues we've found?"

"His name is Chris Kreeger, just like Kris Kringle," Eva said. "And he lived near the North Pole."

"And he knew all the reindeer's names," Winston added.

Ellen nodded. "And he's taking a big trip—"

"And had a list of children he's making presents for," Amy said.

"And he knew what we each wanted for Christmas," Todd reminded them.

"I think he *is* Santa," Lila said softly.

Elizabeth was surprised. Lila had said she didn't believe in Santa Claus before. Now she was changing her mind!

"Elizabeth! Jessica! Your mother's here!" Mrs. Otis called out.

Soon, the party began. There were cupcakes and gingerbread cookies and candy canes. Mrs. Otis explained to everyone what a Hanukkah menorah was for. Then she showed everyone how to play Dreidel. She suggested playing Blind Man's Bluff, while they waited for Chris to arrive. Elizabeth was picked to be blindfolded first.

"Around and around she goes," Mrs. Otis said, turning Elizabeth to confuse her.

Elizabeth kept her eyes closed tight under the scarf. She felt a little bit dizzy from spinning, but started to walk with her arms out.

"Over here, Elizabeth!" someone laughed.

"No, here!"

Elizabeth smiled and waved her arms, trying to catch someone. She walked very slowly and carefully, and tried to recognize people by their voices. But everyone was dodging around her. Then the room became very quiet, and Elizabeth wondered what had happened. Suddenly she bumped into someone.

Her hands touched a wool sleeve with soft fuzzy cuffs. She felt higher and touched a bristly beard. Her heart started pounding. Santa!

Then she remembered Chris and felt silly. "It's Chris," she shouted, taking off her blindfold.

It was Chris, dressed in his Santa suit. Those who had never seen him before stared at him in surprise.

"Ho, ho, ho," Chris said with a laugh. "I guess you couldn't help bumping into someone as roly-poly as I am."

"You look just like Santa Claus!" Caroline Pearce exclaimed.

"You sure do," Ken Matthews said.

Elizabeth looked at the Snoopers. They were the only ones who knew all the clues about Chris. They were the only ones who knew he really might be Santa Claus.

Chris laughed again, and everyone went back to their game.

"Chris?" Elizabeth said in a puzzled voice.

"If you are Santa, why did you come to California?"

He winked at her. "Maybe I wanted to be someplace warm for the winter. It's pretty cold up north, you know. Besides, I like meeting lots of children."

"Chris!" Jessica said. She grabbed her mother's hand and dragged her over to where Chris and Elizabeth were standing. "This is our Mom."

"It's nice to meet you, Mr. Kreeger," Mrs. Wakefield said.

"He's Santa," Jessica whispered.

Mrs. Wakefield smiled. "Jessica thinks you're really Santa Claus," she said with a laugh. "I wish you would tell her you're not."

"Mom!" Elizabeth gasped. Jessica's mouth dropped open.

73

"Next you'll tell me you don't believe in Santa," Chris teased.

Mrs. Wakefield smiled. "Well, let's just say, I don't believe you're Santa Claus."

"Too bad," Chris said, clucking his tongue. "You're never too old to believe."

"Come on, Chris," Jessica cut in. She grabbed Chris's hand. "Let's play some more games." Before Mrs. Wakefield could say anything more, Chris and Jessica walked away.

CHAPTER 11

Santa's Surprise

The party lasted through lunch period. Jessica was starting her third candy cane when Chris said that it was time for him to leave.

"But I have some gifts for you all, including my hostesses," he said, smiling at Mrs. Otis and Mrs. Wakefield.

"You didn't have to do that," Mrs. Otis said.

Chris winked. "I know. But I wanted to. I'll be right back."

Jessica and the other Snoopers gathered

around Mrs. Otis and Mrs. Wakefield. They all looked excited. Jessica wondered what the presents would be. She was sure they would be wonderful.

When Chris came back into the room, he had a sack over his shoulder. He emptied it out and gave each person a small wooden carved animal. Then he took out a big box and a small box. "For you," he said, handing the big box to Mrs. Otis.

"I wonder what this could be," she said, untying the ribbon. She opened the box and gasped.

"A globe!" she said, taking it out. "I was planning to buy one for the classroom. How did you know? That's so thoughtful."

Jessica gulped. Chris had known just what the teacher wanted. She could hardly wait to see what her mother's present was.

"And this one is for you," Chris said, giving the small box to Mrs. Wakefield.

Mrs. Wakefield looked very surprised. "Thank you," she said, taking off the paper. She opened the box slowly, and her expression changed to astonishment. "What—? How—?"

"What is it, Mom?" Elizabeth asked, standing on tiptoe to see.

Mrs. Wakefield's present was a small carved wooden box. There were designs of snowflakes and stars all over it. Mrs. Wakefield was shaking her head from side to side.

"It's exquisite!" she said, almost breathless. "I saw a box just like this when I was a little girl and I wanted it so much. I can't believe this."

The Snoopers all looked at each other with

wide eyes. Only Santa could have known what Mrs. Wakefield wanted as a little girl.

"But I can't keep it," Mrs. Wakefield said. "It must have been very expensive."

"No, not at all," Chris told her with a smile. "I made it myself in my workshop. I made all the carved animals, too."

Jessica felt like jumping for joy. Now her mother would have to believe Chris was Santa, too.

Before Mrs. Wakefield could say anything else, Chris announced he had to get back to work. "Thank you very much for a wonderful party," he said. "I'm glad you invited me."

After Chris left, the room got very quiet.

"Mr. Kreeger is a special person," Mrs. Otis said softly.

Mrs. Wakefield was turning the carved wooden box around and around in her hands.

"How could he possibly have known?" she whispered.

Jessica looked at her sister and smiled. She knew.

CHAPTER 12

Final Proof

The next day was the last day before vacation. During recess, Elizabeth called all the Snoopers together for a meeting.

"Listen, everyone," she said. "We have to find out once and for all if Chris is Santa Claus."

"I'm already positive," Ellen announced.

"Me, too," Winston agreed.

"He knew just what to give Mrs. Otis," Todd scratched his head. "He could have

81

heard that Mrs. Otis wanted a globe," he said, not sounding convinced.

Elizabeth nodded. She was beginning to change her mind, but she wasn't one hundred percent sure. Every single clue indicated that Chris was Santa Claus, but it was hard to believe. Their first mystery was turning out to be difficult.

"Why don't we ask him," Eva suggested.

Everyone looked startled.

"I guess we could," Amy said. "I know he'd tell us the truth, right?"

The others nodded.

"OK," Jessica said. "Let's ask Chris right now."

"Come on," Winston said.

The group raced into the building, down the hall, and came to a halt outside the custodian's office.

"Chris!" Jessica called, knocking on the door.

They waited in silence. Then the door opened. Jim, the usual custodian, was standing there.

"What can I do for you, kids?" he asked. He had a sandwich in his hand, and he took a big bite while he waited.

Elizabeth had a sinking feeling in her stomach. "Where's Chris?" she asked.

"As soon as I came back, he said he had to leave," Jim explained. "He said something about a big job coming up that couldn't wait."

"A big job?" Todd repeated. They all knew what that big job was: delivering presents all over the world.

"Does that mean he's not coming back anymore?" Jessica asked.

83

Jim nodded. "He was just here temporarily while I was sick."

The Snoopers looked at each other. Elizabeth felt very sad all of a sudden. She looked into the office where Chris has been. It seemed empty without him. Then she noticed something on a shelf with the supplies. "Hey," she said. "What's that?"

Elizabeth ran past Jim, and the others followed her. On the shelf was a pair of wire-rimmed glasses and an old clay pipe.

"Well, well, well. Where did those come from?" Jim asked.

Jessica's eyes were round. "They're not yours?"

"No," Jim said. "I guess Chris Kreeger must have left them behind."

Elizabeth stared at the objects. She could

easily imagine Chris in his Santa suit, with the glasses and the pipe.

"We're too late," Todd said quietly.

The group walked down the hall slowly.

"I guess our mystery will be unsolved," Elizabeth said sadly. "We'll never get to ask Chris if he is Santa."

The hallway was crowded and noisy with students going to lunch. Suddenly, in the distance, they heard a familiar sound.

"Ho, ho, ho!"

Elizabeth stopped in her tracks. "It's Chris!" she gasped.

"There he is!" Winston yelled. He pointed down the hallway. Chris was just disappearing around the corner.

"Come on!" Jessica shouted.

The Snoopers started running down the

crowded hall. "Look out!" Todd warned, as they tried not to bump into anyone.

"He's getting away!" Elizabeth said.

They turned the corner and raced for the main door. Just as they burst through, they saw a taxi driving away from school. Elizabeth glimpsed a man with white hair in the back seat.

"There he goes," Ellen wailed.

Elizabeth frowned. "Santa wouldn't leave in a taxi, would he?" she said.

Jessica gave her sister a playful push. She was smiling. "He is Santa, Liz. And you know it."

"We'll never know for sure," Elizabeth said. "But maybe . . ." Elizabeth didn't finish the sentence. She waved as the taxi drove down the road, and remembered Chris's cheerful laugh. He was such a nice man. She

would never know for sure if he was Santa or not, but she knew he had the spirit of Christmas in him. She didn't know if she even believed in Santa Claus again, but deep in her heart she knew it didn't matter.

"I guess we're good detectives," Amy said.

"We sure are," Todd said.

"Case closed," Jessica said with a grin.

The Snoopers all smiled at each other and raced back to Mrs. Otis's class, eager to begin their Christmas vacation.

COULD *YOU* BE THE NEXT SWEET VALLEY READER OF THE MONTH?

ENTER BANTAM BOOKS' SWEET VALLEY CONTEST & SWEEPSTAKES IN ONE!

Calling all Sweet Valley Fans! Here's a chance to appear in a Sweet Valley book!

We know how important Sweet Valley is to you. That's why we've come up with a Sweet Valley celebration offering exciting opportunities to have YOUR thoughts printed in a Sweet Valley book!

"How do I become a Sweet Valley Reader of the Month?"

It's easy. Just write a one-page essay (no more than 150 words, please) telling us a little about yourself, and why you like to read Sweet Valley books. We will pick the best essays and print them along with the winner's photo in the back of upcoming Sweet Valley books. Every month there will be a new Sweet Valley Kids Reader of the Month!

And, there's more!

Just sending in your essay makes you eligible for the Grand Prize drawing for a trip to Los Angeles, California! This once-in-a-life-time trip includes round-trip airfare, accommodations for 5 nights (economy double occupancy), a rental car, and meal allowance. (Approximate retail value: $4,500.)

Don't wait! Write your essay today.
No purchase necessary. See the next page for Official rules.

ENTER BANTAM BOOKS' SWEET VALLEY READER OF THE MONTH SWEEPSTAKES

OFFICIAL RULES:

READER OF THE MONTH ESSAY CONTEST

1. No Purchase Is Necessary. Enter by hand printing your name, address, date of birth and telephone number on a plain 3" x 5" card, and sending this card along with your essay telling us about yourself and why you like to read Sweet Valley books to:

READER OF THE MONTH
SWEET VALLEY KIDS
BANTAM BOOKS
YR MARKETING
666 FIFTH AVENUE
NEW YORK, NEW YORK 10103

2. Reader of the Month Contest Winner. For each month from June 1, 1990 through December 31, 1990, a Sweet Valley Kids Reader of the Month will be chosen from the entries received during that month. The winners will have their essay and photo published in the back of an upcoming Sweet Valley Kids title.

3. Enter as often as you wish, but each essay must be original and each entry must be mailed in a separate envelope bearing sufficient postage. All completed entries must be postmarked and received by Bantam no later than December 31, 1990, in order to be eligible for the Essay Contest and Sweepstakes. Entrants must be between the ages of 6 and 16 years old. Each essay must be no more than 150 words and must be typed double-spaced or neatly printed on one side of an 8 1/2" x 11" page which has the entrant's name, address, date of birth and telephone number at the top. The essays submitted will be judged each month by Bantam's Marketing Department on the basis of originality, creativity, thoughtfulness, and writing ability, and all of Bantam's decisions are final and binding. Essays become the property of Bantam Books and none will be returned. Bantam reserves the right to edit the winning essays for length and readability. Essay Contest winners will be notified by mail within 30 days of being chosen. In the event there are an insufficient number of essays received in any month which meet the minimum standards established by the judges, Bantam reserves the right not to choose a Reader of the Month. Winners have 30 days from the date of Bantam's notice in which to respond, or an alternate Reader of the Month winner will be chosen. Bantam is not responsible for incomplete or lost or misdirected entries.

4. Winners of the Essay Contest and their parents or legal guardians may be required to execute an Affidavit of Eligibility and Promotional Release supplied by Bantam. Entering the Reader of the Month Contest constitutes permission for use of the winner's name, address, likeness and contest submission for publicity and promotional purposes, with no additional compensation.

5. Employees of Bantam Books, Bantam Doubleday Dell Publishing Group, Inc., and their subsidiaries and affiliates, and their immediate family members are not eligible to enter the Essay Contest. The Essay Contest is open to residents of the U.S. and Canada (excluding the province of Quebec), and is void wherever prohibited or restricted by law. All applicable federal, state, and local regulations apply.

READER OF THE MONTH SWEEPSTAKES

6. Sweepstakes Entry. No purchase is necessary. Every entrant in the Sweet Valley High, Sweet Valley Twins and Sweet Valley Kids Essay Contest whose completed entry is received by December 31, 1990 will be entered in the Reader of the Month Sweepstakes. The Grand Prize winner will be selected in a random drawing from all completed entries received on or about February 1, 1991 and will be notified by mail. Bantam's decision is final and binding. Odds of winning are dependent on the number of entries received. The prize is non-transferable and no substitution is allowed. The Grand Prize winner must be accompanied on the trip by a parent or legal guardian. Taxes are the sole responsibility of the prize winner. Trip must be taken within one year of notification and is subject to availability. Travel arrangements will be made for the winner and, once made, no changes will be allowed.

7. 1 Grand Prize. A six day, five night trip for two to Los Angeles, California. Includes round-trip coach airfare, accommodations for 5 nights (economy double occupancy), a rental car – economy model, and spending allowance for meals. (Approximate retail value: $4,500.)

8. The Grand Prize winner and their parent or legal guardian may be required to execute an Affidavit of Eligibility and Promotional Release supplied by Bantam. Entering the Reader of the Month Sweepstakes constitutes permission for use of the winner's name, address, and the likeness for publicity and promotional purposes, with no additional compensation.

9. Employees of Bantam Books, Bantam Doubleday Dell Publishing Group, Inc., and their subsidiaries and affiliates, and their immediate family members are not eligible to enter this Sweepstakes. The Sweepstakes is open to residents of the U.S. and Canada (excluding the province of Quebec), and is void wherever prohibited or restricted by law. If a Canadian resident, the Grand Prize winner will be required to correctly answer an arithmetical skill-testing question in order to receive the prize. All applicable federal, state, and local regulations apply. The Grand Prize will be awarded in the name of the minor's parent or guardian. Taxes, if any, are the winner's sole responsibility.

10. For the name of the Grand Prize winner and the names of the winners of the Sweet Valley High, Sweet Valley Twins and Sweet Valley Kids Essay Contests, send a stamped, self-addressed envelope entirely separate from your entry to: Bantam Books, Sweet Valley Reader of the Month Winners, Young Readers Marketing, 666 Fifth Avenue, New York, New York 10103. The winners list will be available after April 15, 1991.

SWEET VALLEY KIDS

Jessica and Elizabeth have had lots of adventures in *Sweet Valley High* and *Sweet Valley Twins*...now read about the twins at age seven! You'll love all the fun that comes with being seven—birthday parties, playing dress-up, class projects, putting on puppet shows and plays, losing a tooth, setting up lemonade stands, caring for animals and much more! It's all part of SWEET VALLEY KIDS. Read them all!

☐	15681-0	**TEAMWORK #27**	$2.75
☐	15688-8	**APRIL FOOL! #28**	$2.75
☐	15695-0	**JESSICA AND THE BRAT ATTACK #29**	$2.75
☐	15715-9	**PRINCESS ELIZABETH #30**	$2.75
☐	15727-2	**JESSICA'S BAD IDEA #31**	$2.75
☐	15747-7	**JESSICA ON STAGE #32**	$2.75
☐	15753-1	**ELIZABETH'S NEW HERO #33**	$2.75
☐	15766-3	**JESSICA, THE ROCK STAR #34**	$2.75
☐	15772-8	**AMY'S PEN PAL #35**	$2.75
☐	15778-7	**MARY IS MISSING #36**	$2.75
☐	15779-5	**THE WAR BETWEEN THE TWINS #37**	$2.75
☐	15789-2	**LOIS STRIKES BACK #38**	$2.75
☐	15798-1	**JESSICA AND THE MONEY MIX-UP #39**	$2.75
☐	15806-6	**DANNY MEANS TROUBLE #40**	$2.75
☐	15810-4	**THE TWINS GET CAUGHT #41**	$2.75
☐	15824-4	**JESSICA'S SECRET #42**	$2.95
☐	15835-X	**ELIZABETH'S FIRST KISS #43**	$2.95

Bantam Books, Dept. SVT5, 414 East Golf Road, Des Plaines, IL 60016

Please send me the items I have checked above. I am enclosing $_____
(please add $2.00 to cover postage and handling). Send check or money
order, no cash or C.O.D.s please.

Mr/Ms ———————————————————————————————————

Address ——————————————————————————————————

City/State ——————————————————————— Zip ———————————

SVT5-11/90

Please allow four to six weeks for delivery.
Prices and availability subject to change without notice.